JUV/E
PZ
8.1
.P24
Mr
2003

HEGEWI

W9-BYP-719

Mrs. Chicken and the hungry crocodile

HEGEWISCH BRANCH

DISCARD

Mrs. Chicken

AND

THE

Hungry Crocodile

Won-Ldy Paye & Margaret H. Lippert

Illustrated by Julie Paschkis

Henry Holt and Company · NEW YORK

About the Story

Mrs. Chicken and the Hungry Crocodile is a traditional story from the Dan people of northeastern Liberia in Africa. The Dan people are rice farmers who are known for their storytelling, wood carving, masked dancing, and music. Won-Ldy first heard this story from his grandmother Gowo when he was very young.

Henry Holt and Company, LLC / *Publishers since 1866*
115 West 18th Street / New York, New York 10011
www.henryholt.com

Henry Holt is a registered trademark of Henry Holt and Company, LLC
Text copyright © 2003 by Won-Ldy Paye and Margaret H. Lippert. Illustrations copyright © 2003 by Julie Paschkis
All rights reserved.
Distributed in Canada by H. B. Fenn and Company Ltd.

A version of this story was previously published in *Why Leopard Has Spots: Dan Stories from Liberia* by Won-Ldy Paye and Margaret H. Lippert, illustrated by Ashley Bryan, by Fulcrum Publishing, Inc., Golden, Colorado, 1998.

Library of Congress Cataloging-in-Publication Data
Paye, Won-Ldy.
Mrs. Chicken and the hungry crocodile / retold by Won-Ldy Paye and Margaret H. Lippert;
illustrated by Julie Paschkis.
Summary: When a crocodile captures Mrs. Chicken and takes her to an island to fatten her up,
clever Mrs. Chicken claims that she can prove they are sisters and that, therefore, the crocodile
shouldn't eat her.
[1. Dan (African people)—Folklore. 2. Folklore—Liberia. 3. Chickens—Folklore.
4. Crocodiles—Folklore.] I. Lippert, Margaret H. II. Paschkis, Julie, ill. III. Title.
PZ8.1.P24 Mr 2003   398.2'089'9634—dc21   2002001755

ISBN 0-8050-7047-8 / First Edition—2003
The artist used Winsor & Newton gouaches to create the illustrations for this book.
Designed by Martha Rago
Printed in the United States of America on acid-free paper. ∞
10 9 8 7 6 5 4 3

For Matay
—W. P.

For Jocelyn and Dawn
—M. H. L.

For Gus
—J. P.

CHICAGO PUBLIC LIBRARY
HEGEWISCH BRANCH
3048 E. 130TH ST.   608

R0402438821

One morning, Mrs. Chicken took her bath in a puddle.
"Cluck, cluck," she said proudly. "What a pretty
chicken I am! Big, bright eyes. Short, smooth beak.
But I can't see my wings. This puddle is too small."

She walked down to the river to get
a better look.

She didn't know that Crocodile lay in the
river all day long, waiting for her dinner.

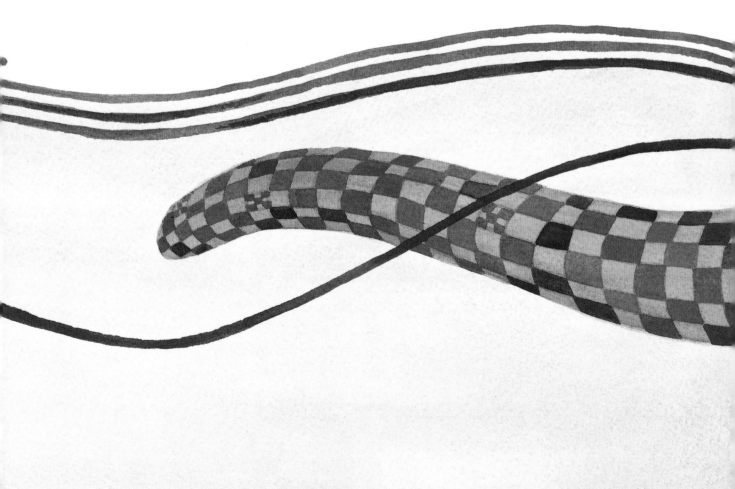

Mrs. Chicken leaned over the water.

"Hmm," she said. "I still can't see my wings. I see scaly green legs. And a long mouth with sharp teeth. But where is my beak?"

Crocodile lay very still and waited. "Yum, yum," she thought. "That's my dinner."

"I look different in the river," said Mrs. Chicken.

She turned to one side. Crocodile did too. Mrs. Chicken turned to the other side. So did Crocodile.

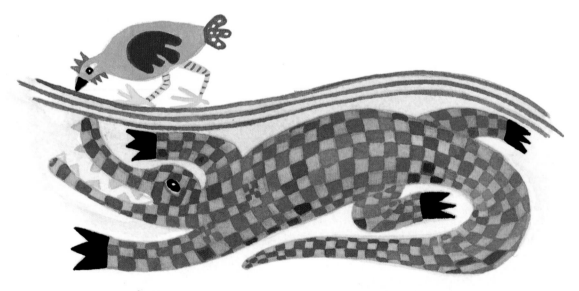

"I'd like a closer look," said Mrs. Chicken. She stepped into the river.

SNAP! Crocodile grabbed Mrs. Chicken's foot in her mouth.

"BOK!"
said Mrs. Chicken.
"Let go!"

Crocodile shook her head. She dragged Mrs. Chicken to her house on the island in the middle of the river. Then she slammed the door shut with her tail and opened her mouth. Mrs. Chicken flew up to the rafters.

"Come down," Crocodile said. "I'm going to eat you up."

"ME?" Mrs. Chicken squawked. "You can't eat me!"

"Ooooh, yes I can," said Crocodile.

"But, " said Mrs. Chicken, "you SHOULDN'T eat me."

"Why not?" asked Crocodile.

"Hawh, hawh, hawh," Crocodile laughed. "You're not my sister. You have speckled feathers. I have green skin. You have a beak. I have a mouth with sharp teeth. And these teeth are going to EAT YOU UP!"

"NO!" said Mrs. Chicken. "We look different. But we're sisters. I'll prove it. Just give me time."

"All right," chuckled Crocodile. "I'll fatten you up. The longer I wait, the plumper you'll get."

Crocodile yawned and curled around her eggs. Soon she was snoring.

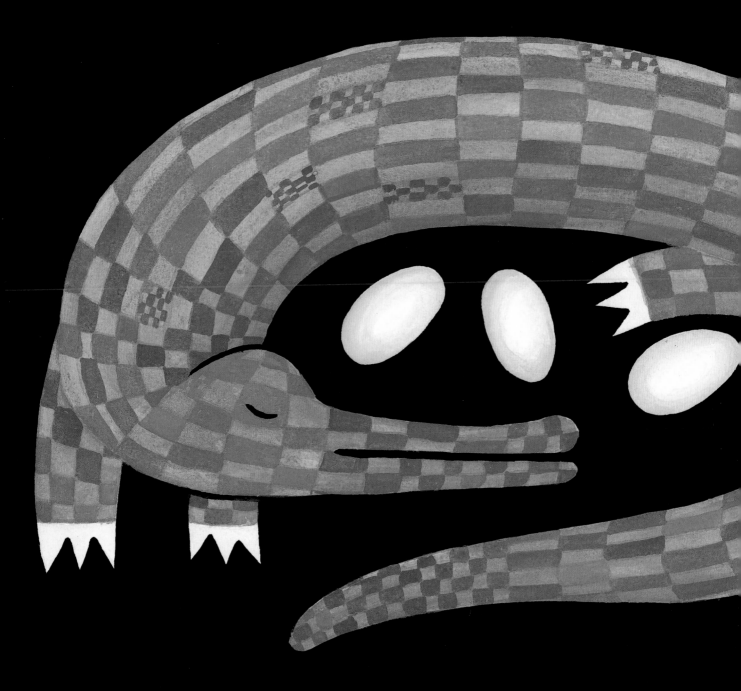

Mrs. Chicken made
a nest in the corner
opposite Crocodile
and settled down
to lay her own eggs.

Every day, Crocodile gave Mrs. Chicken
grain to eat. Every night, they fell
asleep over their eggs. Mrs. Chicken
got fatter and fatter. Crocodile got
thinner and hungrier.

One evening, Crocodile said, "This is your last meal. Tomorrow will be MY big dinner!"

"We'll see," said Mrs. Chicken.

She waited until Crocodile was sleeping.

Then she carefully put her eggs next to Crocodile.

She took Crocodile's eggs to her own nest.

Just before dawn, Crocodile felt something move
beside her.

"Mrs. Chicken!" she called. "Wake up! My babies
are hatching. But why do they have those silly
little beaks and scrawny
little wings?

They look like YOU!"

"My eggs are hatching too," said Mrs. Chicken.
"Look!" She stepped off her nest.

"OH!" said Crocodile.
"What beautiful babies you have! What gorgeous green skin. What lovely long mouths. What darlings.

They look like ME!"

"And your babies look like ME," said Mrs. Chicken. "I TOLD you we're sisters! You almost ATE me! Your own SISTER!"

"I'm really sorry, Sister Chicken," said Crocodile.

"I have an idea," said Mrs. Chicken. "Since you like my babies so much, you can have them. I'll take your funny-looking babies instead."

"Oh, thank you, Sister Chicken," said Crocodile.

"Don't mention it," said Mrs. Chicken. "Sisters help one another."

So they switched babies.

"Time for us to go home now!" Mrs. Chicken said. She and her babies climbed onto Crocodile's back, and Crocodile carried them across the river.

"Bye-bye, Sister," Crocodile said.

Mrs. Chicken waved her wing and hurried her chicks up the riverbank.

"See you soon," called Crocodile.

"No you won't!" called Mrs. Chicken as
she disappeared through the trees.
"Come along, children. Cluck, cluck!"

Since that day, Mrs. Chicken and her children have never gone near the river, and they always take their baths in puddles.

"Big enough for us," Mrs. Chicken tells her children. "And MUCH too small for crocodiles!"